WHY THIS IS AN EASY READER

- This story has been carefully written to keep the young reader's interest high.

- It is told in a simple, open style, with a strong rhythm that adds enjoyment both to reading aloud and silent reading.

- There is a very high percentage of words repeated. It is this skillful repetition which helps the child to read independently. Seeing words again and again, he "practices" the vocabulary he knows, and learns with ease the words that are new.

- Only 204 different words have been used, with plurals and root words counted once.

  86 words—over one-third the total vocabulary—are used at least three times.

  23 words are used at least 10 times.

  Some words have been used 42 times.

ABOUT THIS STORY

- This story reflects the warm feeling of young children for animals. It lends itself to dramatization, to the sharing of experiences about pets, and leads naturally to the further study of animals.

Surprise
in the Tree

Story *by* SARA ASHERON
Pictures *by* SUSAN PERL
Editorial Consultant: LILIAN MOORE

GROSSET & DUNLAP
Publishers
New York, N. Y. 10010

Introduction

These books are meant to help the young reader discover what a delightful experience reading can be. The stories are such fun that they urge the child to try his new reading skills. They are so easy to read that they will encourage and strengthen him as a reader.

The adult will notice that the sentences aren't too long, the words aren't too hard, and the skillful repetition is like a helping hand. What the child will feel is: "This is a good story—and I can read it myself!"

For some children, the best way to meet these stories may be to hear them read aloud at first. Others, who are better prepared to read on their own, may need a little help in the beginning—help that is best given freely. Youngsters who have more experience in reading alone—whether in first or second or third grade—will have the immediate joy of reading "all by myself."

These books have been planned to help all young readers grow—in their pleasure in books and in their power to read them.

Lilian Moore
Specialist in Reading
Formerly of Division of Instructional Research,
New York City Board of Education

Do you think a dog
is the best pet of all?
Jerry did not think so.
Jerry liked cats.

He liked gray cats

and black cats

and white cats.

He liked big cats

and little cats

and fat cats

and skinny cats.

9

The cat he liked best of all
lived across the street.
She was a big yellow cat,
and her name was Amanda.

One day Amanda had kittens.

One kitten was all white.

Two kittens were gray
and white.

But one of the kittens
was a little yellow ball
of fur — just like Amanda.

That was the kitten Jerry wanted
most of all.
And that was the kitten his mother
said he could keep for his very own!

Jerry told his kitten
a secret.
"Next to my mother and
father," he said, "I think
I love you the most."
The kitten just purred,
as if to say, "I know!"

15

One day Jerry's mother said,
"Guess what your cat makes me
think of?"
"I give up!" said Jerry.
"A penny," said his mother.
"A bright new penny!"
Jerry laughed.
"Penny! That's what I'll
call you!" he told his kitten.
And that's how Penny
got her name.

Penny was a very busy kitten.
She was into things
and under things
all the time.

18

One day Jerry's mother found
Penny in her new hat.
"What in the world
will you do next?" she said.

This is what Penny did next!

And this!

Honey

Raspb

Coo Kies

Jam

JEL

And then one day
Penny fell into the tub
when Jerry was taking a bath!

"That cat!" said Jerry's mother.

"Look at her!

She is into everything!"

Jerry laughed.

"She wants to find out about

everything," he told his mother.

"I think she wants to find out

what the world is like."

Every day, when Jerry came home
from school, he looked for Penny.
And every day, there she was,
waiting for him.

Every day, after school, they had
milk and cookies together.

One day, when Jerry came home
from school, he did not see Penny
at the window.

"Where's Penny?"

he asked his mother.

"I let her out," his mother said.

"I guess she has not come back yet."

Jerry ran outside.

"Here, Penny!" he called.

"Here, Penny!"

Penny was not in the basket.

Penny was not under the steps.

Penny was not in the tall grass.

Where was his kitten?

Jerry ran down the street.

"Here, Penny!" he called
again and again. "Here, Penny!"
Meow! Meow!
Was that Penny?

Meow!

Yes—it was his kitten!

Jerry looked around,

but he did not see her.

"Meow! Meow!"

cried Penny again.

Jerry looked up.

There was Penny—

way up in a tree.

35

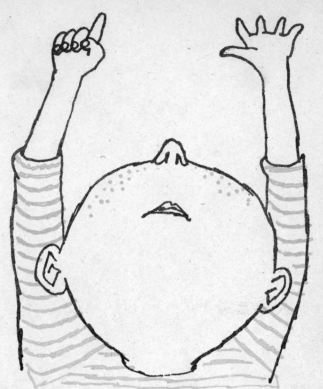

"Meow!" cried Penny. "Meow!"
Jerry could see
how scared she was.
He called up to her,
"It's all right, Penny.
I'm going for help,
and I'll be right back!"

Jerry ran up the street
to his house.

"Mom! Mom!" he cried.

"Penny is way up in a tree,
and she's too scared
to come down!"

Jerry's mother went
at once to get a ladder.
Then she saw the tree.
"Oh no!" she said.
"This ladder will never do!"

"Meow!" cried Penny.

"Meow! Meow!"

"Oh Mom!" said Jerry.

"She's so scared!

I can tell.

Do something!"

Jerry's mother looked up

at Penny.

"I'll call the Fire Department,"

she said.

"They will come

and get her down."

Jerry's mother called
the Fire Department right away.
"Our kitten is up
in a tree," she said.
"Can you help us
get her down?"

"We will come as soon as we can,"
the fireman said.

Soon?

It did not seem very soon to Jerry.

He stood under the tree,

feeling more and more unhappy.

"Meow! Meow!"

Penny called and called.

And it seemed to Jerry

that she was calling,

"Get me down!

I'm scared, up here!"

Jerry could not wait.

He *had* to help his kitten.

He began to climb the tree.

"Don't be scared, Penny,"
he called to her.

"Here I come!"
Jerry climbed up
as far as he could go.
But he could not
get up to Penny.

And now he could not get down!

Penny looked down at Jerry.

She liked having him in the tree.

Now she was not so scared.

She stood up and looked around.

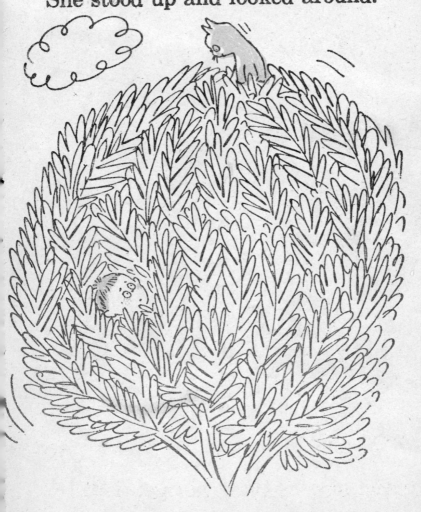

She looked down at the next tree.

She took one step—

then another.

Then she jumped into the other tree
and ran down.

Clang! Clang!

The fire truck was coming

down the street.

Jerry's mother ran out

to meet the firemen.

"This way!" she cried.

"Our cat is up in this tree."

The firemen took a big ladder
and ran to the tree.

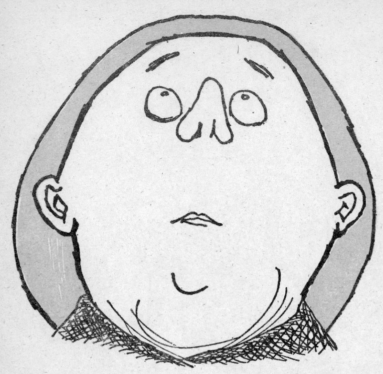

One fireman looked up at the tree.

"Does your cat wear blue jeans?"

the fireman asked.

Jerry's mother looked up, too.

"Jerry!" she cried. "What are *you*

doing up there?"

"I can't get down," said Jerry.

"Meow!" cried Penny.

Jerry's mother looked down.

"And what are *you*

doing down here?" she said.

"Meow!" cried Penny, as if to say,

"Come! Come!

Get my boy down from that tree!"

The fireman began
to climb the ladder.
"I will have to hurry," he said,
"before the cat goes up
to get the boy
who went up
to get the cat!"

"Hello, Jerry!"

said the fireman.

"How do you like it up here?"

"Not so very much," said Jerry.

"Hold on, then," said the fireman.

"Let's go!"

And down the ladder he came
with Jerry.

"Thank you!" said Jerry.

"You're welcome!" said the fireman.

"It's not every day I climb up to get
a cat out of a tree and come down
with a boy instead!"